Astrid
Lindgren

The Amazing Pippi
Longstocking

PENGUIN BOOKS

PENGUIN BOOKS

Published by the Penguin Group
Penguin Books Ltd, 27 Wrights Lane, London w8 5tz, England
Penguin Books USA Inc., 375 Hudson Street, New York, New York 10014, USA
Penguin Books Australia Ltd, Ringwood, Victoria, Australia
Penguin Books Canada Ltd, 10 Alcorn Avenue, Toronto, Ontario, Canada m4v 3b2
Penguin Books (NZ) Ltd, 182–190 Wairau Road, Auckland 10, New Zealand

Penguin Books Ltd, Registered Offices: Harmondsworth, Middlesex, England

First published in *Pippi Longstocking* by Rabén & Sjögren 1945
English translation first published by Oxford University Press 1954
Published in Puffin Books 1976

This collection published in Penguin Books 1996
3 5 7 9 10 8 6 4 2

Copyright 1945 by Astrid Lindgren
Translation copyright 1954 by Oxford University Press
All rights reserved

Set in 11.5/13.5pt Bembo Monotype
Typeset by Datix International Limited, Bungay, Suffolk
Printed in England by Clays Ltd, St Ives plc

Contents

Pippi Comes to Villekulla Cottage

At the end of a little Swedish town lay an old, over-grown orchard. In the orchard was a cottage, and in this cottage lived Pippi Longstocking. She was nine years old, and she lived all alone. She had neither mother nor father, which was really rather nice, for in this way there was no one to tell her to go to bed just when she was having most fun, and no one to make her take cod-liver-oil when she felt like eating peppermints.

There was a time when Pippi had had a father, and she had been very fond of him. Of course, she had had a mother too, but that was long ago.

Pippi's mother had died when Pippi was just a tiny baby lying in her cradle and howling so dreadfully that no one could come near. Pippi believed that her mother now lived somewhere up in Heaven and looked down on her little girl through a hole in it. Pippi often used to wave up to her and say, 'Don't worry, I can look after myself!'

Pippi hadn't forgotten her father. He had been a ship's captain, and sailed on the great ocean. Pippi had sailed with him on his boat, at least until the time he had blown into the sea during a storm and disappeared. But Pippi was quite sure that one day he would come back, for she never believed that he had drowned. She was certain that he had come ashore on a desert island, one with lots and lots of cannibals, and that her father had become king of them all and went about all day with a gold crown on his head.

'*My* father is a Cannibal King; there aren't *many* children with so fine a father!' said Pippi, really pleased with herself. 'And when my father has built himself a boat he'll come to fetch me, and then *I* shall become a Cannibal Princess. What a life it will be!'

Her father had bought the old cottage in the orchard many years ago. He had wanted to live there with Pippi when he grew old and sailed the seas no longer. But then he had unfortunately been blown into the sea, and as Pippi expected him to return she went straight home to Villekulla Cottage, as their house was called. It stood there furnished and ready and waiting for her. One fine summer's evening she had said good-bye to all the sailors on her father's boat. They liked Pippi very much, and Pippi liked them.

'Good-bye, boys!' said Pippi, kissing each in turn on the forehead. 'Don't worry about me. I can take care of myself!'

She took two things from the boat, a little monkey whose name was Mr Nelson (he had been a present from her father) and a big suitcase full of gold pieces. The sailors stood by the rail and watched Pippi until she was out of sight. She kept on walking without turning round once, with Mr Nelson on her shoulder and the suitcase firmly in her hand.

'A remarkable child,' said one of the sailors, wiping a tear from his eye when Pippi disappeared from view.

He was right. Pippi was a very remarkable child, and the most remarkable thing about her was her strength. She was *so* strong that in all the world there was no policeman as strong as she. She could have lifted a whole horse if she had wanted to. And there were times when she *did* want to. Pippi had bought a horse of her very own with one of her gold pieces the day she came home to Villekulla Cottage. She had always longed to have her very own horse, and now there was one living on her front porch. When Pippi wanted to take afternoon tea there, she simply lifted him out into the orchard without further ado.

Next to Villekulla Cottage lay another orchard and another house. In that house lived a mother and a father with their two nice little children, a boy and a girl. The boy's name was Tommy and the girl's Annika. They were both very good and well-brought-up and obedient children. Tommy *never* bit his nails, and *always* did what his mother asked. Annika *never* fussed when she didn't get her own way, and she was always very properly dressed in freshly ironed cotton.

Tommy and Annika played nicely together in their orchard, but they had often wished for a playmate. At the time when Pippi always sailed the seas with her father, they would sometimes hang on the fence and say to each other, 'What a pity no one moves into that house! Someone ought to live there; someone with children.'

The beautiful summer's day that Pippi first crossed the threshold of Villekulla Cottage, Tommy and Annika weren't at home. They were spending the week with their grandmother, and so had no idea 4 that someone had moved into the house next to theirs. The first day after their arrival home they stood by the gate and looked out on the street, and they still didn't know that there was a playmate so near. Just as they stood and wondered what they should do, and if possibly anything *special* would happen that day or if it would be just one of those dull days when one couldn't think of anything in particular to do, why, just then the gate to Villekulla Cottage opened and a little girl appeared. She was the most curious child Tommy and Annika had ever seen. It was Pippi Longstocking going for a morning walk. This is what she looked like:

Her hair was the same colour as a carrot, and was braided in two stiff pigtails that stood straight out from her head. Her nose was the shape of a very small potato, and was dotted with freckles. Under the nose was a really very large mouth, with healthy white teeth. Her dress was curious indeed. Pippi had made it herself. It was supposed to have been blue, but as there hadn't been quite enough blue cloth, Pippi had decided to add little red patches here and there. On her long thin legs she wore long stockings, one brown and the other black. And she had a pair of black shoes which were just twice as long as her feet. 5

Her father had bought them in South America so she would have something to grow into, and Pippi never wanted any others.

The thing that made Tommy and Annika open their eyes widest was the monkey which sat on the strange girl's shoulder. It was little and long-tailed, and dressed in blue trousers, yellow jacket, and a white straw hat.

Pippi went on down the street, walking with one foot on the pavement and the other in the gutter. Tommy and Annika watched her until she was out of sight. In a moment she returned, walking backwards. This was so she shouldn't have to take the trouble to turn round when she went home. When she came level with Tommy and Annika's gate, she stopped. The children looked at each other in silence. At last Tommy said, 'Why are you walking backwards?'

'Why am I walking backwards?' said Pippi. 'This is a free country, isn't it? Can't I walk as I please? Why, let me tell you that in Egypt *everyone* walks that way, and no one thinks it the least bit odd.'

'How do you know that?' asked Tommy. 'You haven't been in Egypt, have you ?'

'Have I been to Egypt! You can bet your boots I

have. I've been all over the world and seen odder things than people who walk backwards. I wonder what you would have said if I'd walked on my hands like the people do in Indo-China?'

'That can't be true,' protested Tommy.

Pippi considered this for a moment. 'Yes, you're right,' she said sadly, 'I wasn't telling the truth.'

'It's wicked to lie,' said Annika, who at last had found her tongue.

'Yes, it's *very* wicked,' said Pippi, even more sadly. 'But I forget once in a while, you see. How can you expect a little child whose mother is an angel and whose father is a Cannibal King and who has spent her life sailing the seas to tell the truth always? And for that matter,' she said, a smile spreading over her whole freckled face, 'I can tell you that in the Belgian Congo there isn't a single person who tells the truth. They tell fibs all day and every day, begin at seven in the morning and keep it up until sunset. So if I should happen to tell a fib sometimes you must try to forgive me and remember that it's only because I've been a little too long in the Belgian Congo. We can still be friends, can't we?'

'Of course?' said Tommy, realizing suddenly that this *wouldn't* be one of those dull days.

'Why not have breakfast at my house, for that matter?' Pippi wondered.

'Well, yes,' said Tommy, 'why not? Come on, let's!'

'Yes,' said Annika. 'Right away!'

'But first let me introduce you to Mr Nelson,' said Pippi. The monkey raised his hat to them politely.

And so they went through Villekulla Cottage's tumble-down orchard gate and up the path between rows of mossy trees (trees lovely for climbing, they noticed) to the house and on to the porch. There stood the horse, munching oats from a soup tureen.

'Why on earth have you a horse on the front porch?' asked Tommy. All the horses he knew lived in stables.

'Well,' said Pippi after thinking it over, 'he'd be in the way in the kitchen, and he doesn't thrive in the parlour.'

Tommy and Annika patted the horse, and then went on into the house. There was a kitchen and a parlour and a bedroom. But it looked as if Pippi had forgotten to turn out the rooms that week. Tommy and Annika looked carefully about in case that Cannibal King should be in a corner. They'd never seen a

Cannibal King in all their lives. But no father was to be seen, nor any mother, and Annika asked anxiously, 'Do you live here all alone?'

'Of course not,' said Pippi, 'Mr Nelson lives here too.'

'Yes, but haven't you a mother and father here?'

'No, none at all,' said Pippi cheerfully.

'But who tells you when to go to bed at night, and that sort of thing?' asked Annika.

'I do,' said Pippi. 'The first time I say it, I say it in a friendly sort of way, and if I don't listen I say it again more sharply, and if I *still* don't listen, then there's a thrashing to be had, believe me!'

Tommy and Annika didn't quite understand all this, but they thought that perhaps it was a good arrangement. Meanwhile, they had come into the kitchen, and Pippi whooped:

> 'Here pancakes will be baked now,
> Here pancakes will be served now,
> Here pancakes will be fried now!'

At which she took out three eggs and flung them into the air. One of the eggs fell on her head and broke, and the yolk ran down into her eye. But the 9 others she caught properly in a bowl, where they broke.

'I've always heard that egg-yolk is good for the hair,' said Pippi, wiping her eye. 'You'll see that it will grow now so fast it creaks! In Brazil, for that matter, *everyone* goes about with egg in his hair. There's not a bald head to be seen. Once there was an old man who was so odd that he *ate* his eggs instead of spreading them on his hair. He turned quite bald, too, and when he as much as showed himself on the streets the traffic stopped and they had to call out the police.'

While she was talking, Pippi carefully picked out all the broken eggshell from the bowl with her fingers. Then she took a bath-brush which hung on the wall and began beating the batter so that it splattered on the walls. At last she threw what was left on a griddle that stood on the stove. When the pancake was browned on one side she threw it halfway to the ceiling so that it turned in the air and was caught in the pan again. And when it was done, she threw it across the kitchen so that it landed on a plate standing on the table.

10   'Eat it!' she cried. 'Eat it before it gets cold!'

Tommy and Annika ate, and thought it a very good pancake. Afterwards, Pippi invited them into the parlour. There was only one piece of furniture in it. It was an enormous cupboard with many, many little drawers. Pippi opened them one by one and showed Tommy and Annika all the treasures she kept there. There were strange birds' eggs, and unusual shells and stones, lovely little boxes, beautiful silver mirrors, a pearl necklace, and much more, all bought by Pippi and her father during their travels round the world. Pippi gave her new playmates each a little present as a keepsake. Tommy's was a knife with a gleaming mother-of-pearl handle, and Annika's a little box decorated on the lid with pieces of shell. In the box lay a ring set with a green stone.

'If you should happen to go home now,' said Pippi, 'you'll be able to come again tomorrow. Because if you don't go home, you can't very well come back, and that *would* be a shame.'

Tommy and Annika thought so too, so they went home. They went past the horse, who had eaten up all his oats, and out through the gate of Villekulla Cottage. Mr Nelson waved his hat to them as they left.

Pippi is a Turnupstuffer and Gets into a Fight

ANNIKA awoke especially early the next morning. She bounded out of bed and quickly padded over to Tommy.

'Wake up, Tommy!' she said, tugging at his arm. 'Let's go and see that funny girl with the big shoes!'

In an instant, Tommy was wide awake.

'All the time I was sleeping I knew there was going to be something nice about today, though I couldn't remember just what it was,' he said, struggling out of his pyjama-top. Then they both went into the bathroom and washed themselves and brushed their teeth much faster than usual. They were merry and quick about putting on their clothes, and a whole hour earlier than their mother had expected they came sliding down the banister from the top floor and landed exactly by the breakfast table, where they sat down and shouted that they wanted their hot chocolate now, at *once*!

'And may I ask,' said their mother, 'just what it is that makes you in such a hurry?'

'We're going over to see the new girl in the house next door,' said Tommy.

'We might stay all day!' added Annika.

That morning Pippi was baking ginger-snaps. She had made a huge pile of dough, and was rolling it out on the kitchen floor.

''Cause can you imagine,' said Pippi to her little monkey, 'what earthly good a pastry board would be when you're going to make at least five hundred ginger-snaps?'

There she lay on the floor and cut out heart-shaped ginger-snaps as if her life depended on it.

'Do stop walking in the dough, Mr Nelson,' she said irritably just as the doorbell rang.

Pippi ran to open it. She was as white as a miller from top to toe, and when she shook hands heartily with Tommy and Annika a whole cloud of flour came down on them.

'How nice of you to drop in,' she said, shaking a new cloud of flour out of her apron. Tommy and Annika got so much of it in their throats, they had to cough.

'What are you doing?' asked Tommy.

'Well, if I say I'm sweeping the chimney you 13

wouldn't believe me, as clever as you are,' said Pippi. 'As a matter of fact, I'm baking. But that will soon be out of the way. You can sit on the woodbox in the meantime.'

Pippi could work *very* fast. Tommy and Annika sat on the woodbox and watched how she cut her way forward through the dough, and how she threw the biscuits on to the tins, and how she slung the tins into the oven. They thought it was all rather like something in the films.

'All clear,' said Pippi at last, slamming the oven door after the last tins with a bang.

'What are we going to do now?' asked Tommy.

'I don't know what *you're* thinking of doing,' said Pippi, 'but as for me, I'm not one who can take things easy. I happen to be a turnupstuffer, so of course I never have a free moment.'

'What did you say you were?' asked Annika.

'A turnupstuffer.'

'What's that?' asked Tommy.

'Somebody who finds the stuff that turns up if only you look, of course. What else would it be?' said Pippi, sweeping together all the flour on the floor into a little pile. 'The whole world is filled with things that are just waiting for someone to come along and find them, and that's just what a turnup-stuffer does.'

'What sort of things?' asked Annika.

'Oh, *all* sorts,' said Pippi. 'Gold nuggets and ostrich feathers and dead mice and rubber bands and tiny little grouse, and *that* kind of thing.'

Tommy and Annika thought it sounded a great deal of fun, and at once wanted to become turnup-stuffers too, though Tommy said he hoped he would find a gold nugget and not a little grouse.

'We'll have to wait and see,' said Pippi. 'You always find *something*. But we'll have to hurry up so other turnupstuffers don't come first and take away all the gold nuggets and things that are waiting hereabouts.'

The three turnupstuffers set out. They thought it was best to begin hunting around the houses in the neighbourhood, because Pippi said that even if there *were* little grouse deep in the woods, the *very* best things were almost always found near where people lived.

'Though not always,' she said. 'I've seen it just the other way about. I remember a time when I was looking for things in the jungles of Borneo. Right in 15 the middle of the wild jungle, where no man had ever put his foot, what do you suppose I found? A lovely wooden leg! I gave it away later on to an old man who was one-legged, and he told me that money couldn't buy a wooden leg like that!'

Tommy and Annika watched Pippi to see how a turnupstuffer should act. She ran from one side of the road to the other, shading her eyes with her hand, and searching and searching. Once in a while she crept on her knees, and stuck her hands in through a fence, saying in a disappointed voice, 'Strange! I was *sure* I saw a gold nugget!'

'Can you really take anything you find?' asked Annika.

'Yes, anything that's lying on the ground,' said Pippi.

A little farther on, an old man lay sleeping on the lawn in front of his house.

'*That's* lying on the ground,' said Pippi, 'and we've found him. We'll take him!'

Tommy and Annika were horrified.

'No, no, Pippi! We can't take a gentleman! That would never do!' said Tommy. 'Anyway, what would 16 we do with him?'

'What we'd do with him? We could use him for *lots* of things. We could keep him in a little rabbit hutch instead of a rabbit, and feed him dandelion leaves. But if you don't want to, we can leave him here, for all I care. Still, I hate to think that some other turnupstuffer may come along and carry him off.'

They went on. Suddenly, Pippi gave a wild shriek.

'Well, I never saw the likes!' she cried, picking up an old rusty cake tin out of the grass. 'What a find! What a find! One can never have too many tins.'

Tommy looked rather suspiciously at the tin and asked, 'What can you use that for?'

'It can be used for *lots* of things,' said Pippi. 'One way is to put cakes in it. Then it will be one of those nice Tins With Cakes. Another way is *not* to put cakes in it. Then it will be a Tin Without Cakes, which isn't quite as nice, but it would do well enough too.'

She inspected the tin, which really was quite rusty, and had a hole in the bottom.

'It looks as though this one is a Tin Without Cakes,' she said thoughtfully. 'But you can put it over your head and pretend it's the middle of the night!' 17

And she did just that. With the tin over her head, she wandered through the neighbourhood like a little tin tower, and she didn't stop before she fell on her stomach over a wire fence. There was a terrific crash when the cake tin hit the ground.

'There, you see!' said Pippi, removing the tin. 'If I hadn't had this on me, I would have fallen face first and knocked myself silly.'

'Yes, but,' said Annika, 'if you hadn't had the tin on you, why, you'd never have tripped over the fence . . .'

But before she had finished speaking, another shriek came from Pippi, who triumphantly held up an empty cotton reel.

'It seems to be my lucky day today!' she said. 'What a perfectly sweet little reel to blow soap bubbles with, or to hang on a string round my neck for a necklace! I want to go home and do it now.'

Just then, the gate to a near-by house opened, and a little boy rushed out. He looked frightened, which wasn't surprising, for hard on his heels came five other boys. They soon got hold of him and pushed 18 him against the fence, where the whole lot attacked him. All five began hitting him at the same time. He cried and tried to shield his face with his arms.

'On him, blokes!' yelled the biggest and the strongest of the boys. 'So he'll never dare show himself in *this* street!'

'Oh!' said Annika. 'That's Willie they're beating. How can they be so horrid!'

'It's that beastly Bengt. He's always fighting,' said Tommy. 'And five against one! What cowards!'

Pippi went up to the boys and tapped Bengt on the back with her finger.

'You there,' she said. 'Do you mean to make pulp of little Willie on the spot, since five of you are at him at once?'

Bengt turned round and saw a girl he'd never met before, an unruly, strange girl who dared to poke him! At first he simply stared in astonishment, and then a broad sneer spread over his face.

'Hey, blokes!' he said. 'Let Willie go, and take a look at this. What a girl!'

He slapped his knees and laughed. In a moment the whole lot had flocked around Pippi. Everyone except Willie, who dried his tears and carefully went and stood beside Tommy.

'Have you ever seen such hair! It's a real flaming bonfire! And what shoes!' Bengt continued. 'Couldn't I please borrow one of them? I'd like to go for a row, and I haven't a boat.'

Then he took hold of one of Pippi's pigtails, but quickly dropped it and said, 'Ouch! I burned myself!'

The five boys made a ring round Pippi and hopped about and yelled, 'Carrot top! Carrot top!'

Pippi stood in the middle of the ring and smiled in a friendly manner. Bengt had hoped she would become angry or begin to cry. At the very least she ought to look scared. When nothing else worked, he pushed her.

'I don't think you have particularly good manners with ladies,' said Pippi. Then she lifted him high into the air with her strong arms. She carried him to a near-by birch tree, and hung him across a branch. Then she took the next boy and hung him on another branch, and then she took the next one and sat him on the high gatepost outside the house, and then she took the *next* one and threw him right over the fence, leaving him sitting in a bed of flowers in the next-door garden. She put the last of the bullies into a little toy cart that stood on the road. Then Pippi and Tommy and Annika and Willie stood looking at the boys a while, and the bullies were quite speechless with astonishment.

Pippi said, 'You are cowards! Five of you go after one boy. That's cowardly. And then you begin to push a little defenceless girl around. Oh, how disgraceful! Nasty!'

'Come on now, let's go home,' she said to Tommy and Annika. And to Willie she said, 'If they try 'n hit you any more, just tell me about it.'

And to Bengt, who sat up in the tree and didn't dare to move, she said, 'If there's anything else you wanted to say about my hair or my shoes, it's best you see to it now, before I go home.'

But Bengt hadn't anything else to say about Pippi's shoes, nor about her hair. And so Pippi took her cake tin in one hand and the cotton reel in the other, and went off, followed by Tommy and Annika.

When they came back to Pippi's orchard, Pippi said, 'Dear hearts, what a shame. Here I've found two such fine things and you haven't found anything at all. You must look a little more. Tommy, why don't you look in that old tree? Old trees are often the very best of places for a turnupstuffer.'

Tommy said that he didn't really think that Annika and he would ever be able to find anything, but in order to please Pippi, he stuck his hand down a hollow in the tree.

'Well but –' he said, quite amazed, and pulled out his hand. Between his thumb and forefinger he held a fine notebook with a leather cover. There was a silver pen in a special holder at the side.

'Gosh! That was odd,' said Tommy.

'There, you see!' said Pippi. 'There's nothing better than being a turnupstuffer. It's only a wonder that there aren't more who take up the work. Carpenter and shoemaker and chimney sweep and that sort of thing, *that* they'll become, but turnupstuffer, mark you, that's not good enough!'

And then she said to Annika, 'Why don't you go and feel in that old tree stump? You can just about *always* find things in old tree stumps.'

Annika stuck her hand under the stump, and almost right away got hold of a red coral necklace.

22 Tommy and she just stood and gaped, they were so

surprised. They decided that from now on they were going to be turnupstuffers *every* day.

Pippi had been up half the night tossing a ball, so now she suddenly felt sleepy.

'I think I'll go in and have a bit of a snooze,' she said. 'Won't you come along and tuck me in?'

When Pippi sat on the edge of the bed taking off her shoes, she looked thoughtfully at them and said, 'He wanted to go rowing, that Bengt said. Bosh!' she snorted scornfully. 'I'll teach *him* to row, I will! Some other time.'

'I say, Pippi,' said Tommy cautiously, 'why is it you've got such big shoes?'

'Why, so I can wiggle my toes!' she answered. Then she lay down to sleep. She always slept with her feet on the pillow and her head far down under the covers.

'That's the way they sleep in Guatemala,' she explained. 'And it's the only right way to do it. This way, I can wiggle my toes while I'm sleeping, too.

'Can you go to sleep without a lullaby?' she continued. 'I always have to sing to me for a while, else I can't get a wink of sleep.'

Tommy and Annika heard a droning from under 23

the covers. It was Pippi singing herself to sleep. They tiptoed softly out so they shouldn't disturb her. At the door they turned round and took a last look at the bed. They didn't see anything except Pippi's feet on the pillow. There she lay, wiggling her toes energetically.

Tommy and Annika bounded home. Annika clutched her coral necklace tightly in her hand.

'It *was* odd,' she said. 'Tommy, you don't think . . . do you, that Pippi had already put the things there herself?'

'You can't tell,' said Tommy. 'You can't really be certain about *anything* when it comes to Pippi.'

Pippi Plays Tag with Policemen

EVERYONE in the town soon knew that a little girl just nine years old was living alone in Villekulla Cottage. Mothers and fathers shook their heads and agreed that this would not do at *all*. Certainly all children had to have someone to tell them what they ought to do, and all children ought to go to school to learn the multiplication tables. And so they decided that the little girl in Villekulla Cottage should be put into a Children's Home at once.

One beautiful afternoon Pippi had invited Tommy and Annika to her house for tea and ginger-snaps. She set the tea things out on the steps of the front porch. It was sunny and pretty there, and the flowers in Pippi's garden smelled sweetly. Mr Nelson climbed up and down the porch railing, and now and again the horse would stick his nose forward expecting to be offered a ginger-snap.

'How lovely it is to be alive!' and Pippi, stretching her legs out as far as they would go.

Just then two policemen in full uniform came in through the gate.

25

'Oh!' said Pippi. 'This must be my lucky day, too! Policemen are the very best thing I know. Except for strawberries and cream.'

And she went forward to meet the policemen, her face shining with delight.

'Are you the girl who's moved into Villekulla Cottage?' asked one of the policemen.

'Not me!' said Pippi. 'I'm her very small aunt who lives on the third floor at the other end of the town.'

She only said this because she wanted to have a bit of fun with the policemen. But they didn't think it was the least bit funny. They told her not to try to be so clever. And then they explained that kind people in the town had arranged for her to be placed in a Children's Home.

'I'm already in a Children's Home,' said Pippi.

'What's that? Is it already arranged?' asked the policeman. 'Which Children's Home is that?'

'*This* one,' said Pippi proudly. 'I'm a child, and this is my home. There aren't any grown-ups living here, so I think that makes it a Children's Home.'

'Dear child,' said the policeman, laughing, 'you don't understand. You must come to a regular Institution where someone can look after you.'

'Are horses allowed in the stintitution?' wondered Pippi.

'No, of course not,' said the policeman.

'That's that, I suppose. I thought as much,' said Pippi gloomily. 'Well, how about monkeys, then?'

'Certainly not! I should think you'd know that.'

'I see,' said Pippi. 'Then you'll just have to find yourself kids for that stintitution of yours somewhere else. 'Cause *I* don't mean to move there.'

'Yes, but don't you see, you have to go to school,' said the policeman.

'Why do I?'

'Well, to learn things, of course.'

'What kind of things?' Pippi asked.

'Any number of different kinds,' said the policeman. 'A whole lot of useful things, multiplication tables, for example.'

'I've managed well enough without any pluttification tables for nine years,' said Pippi. 'So I s'pose I can keep managing.'

'Come now! Imagine how unpleasant it will be for you to be so ignorant. Just think, when you grow up and someone perhaps comes and asks you what the capital of Portugal is, you couldn't answer.'

27

'Oh, yes I could,' said Pippi. 'I'd just say, "If you're all that anxious to know what the capital of Portugal is, well, by all means write direct to Portugal and ask 'em."'

'Yes, but don't you think you'd be sorry you didn't know it yourself?'

'Might be so,' said Pippi. 'I s'pose I *would* lie awake sometimes at night and wonder and wonder, "What the dickens was the name of the capital of Portugal?" But then, you can't have fun *all* the time,' said Pippi, turning a few cartwheels. 'Anyway, I've been in Lisbon with my father,' she continued while upside-down and then right-side-up, for she could talk that way too.

But then one of the policemen said that Pippi shouldn't believe that she could do exactly as she pleased. She would just come along to the Children's Home, and that at *once*. He went towards her and took hold of her arm. But Pippi quickly slipped loose, hit him lightly, and said, 'Tag!' And before he could blink his eyes, she had taken a leap up the post of the porch. With a few pulls she was up on the balcony over the porch. The policemen didn't feel inclined to climb after her the same way, so they rushed into the house and up to the first floor. But when they came out on the balcony, Pippi was already halfway to the roof. She climbed on the roof-tiles very much as if she herself were a monkey. In a moment she stood on the top of the roof and jumped easily up on to the chimney. Down on the balcony both the policemen stood tearing their hair, and on the lawn below stood Tommy and Annika looking up at Pippi.

'What fun it is to play tag!' shouted Pippi. 'And how nice it was of you to come. It's my lucky day today too, that's plain to see.'

When the policemen had thought a moment they went and got a ladder which they leaned against the roof, and then they climbed up, first one and then the other, to fetch Pippi down. But they looked a little bit afraid when they climbed out on to the top of the roof and began balancing their way towards Pippi.

'Don't be scared!' cried Pippi. 'It's not dangerous – just fun!'

When the policemen came within two steps of Pippi, she leaped quickly down from the chimney, and laughing and whooping, ran along the top of the roof to the other gable. A few yards from the house stood a tree.

'Watch me dive!' shouted Pippi, and then she hopped straight down into the tree's green crown, hung fast in a branch, dangled back and forth a moment, and let herself fall to the ground. And then she dashed off on to the other gable and took away the ladder.

The policemen had looked a bit foolish when Pippi jumped, but they looked even more so when they had balanced their way back along the top of the roof and wanted to climb down the ladder. At first they became dreadfully angry and yelled at Pippi, who stood below looking up at them, that she'd better put the ladder back, or else they'd show her a thing or two.

'Why are you so angry?' said Pippi reproachfully. 'We're only playing tag, so we all ought to be friends!'

The policemen thought for a moment, and at last one of them said in a small voice, 'Um, err, I say, wouldn't you be nice and bring the ladder back so that we can get down?'

30   'Certainly I will,' said Pippi, and brought the

ladder back at once. 'And then we can have tea and have a nice time together!'

But the policemen were very deceitful, to be sure, for as soon as they were on the ground they rushed upon Pippi and shouted, 'Now you're going to get it, you nasty child!'

But then Pippi said, 'No, now I haven't time to play any longer. Though it *is* fun, I must admit.'

Then she took a strong hold of their belts, and carried them along the orchard, and out through the gate to the road. There she set them down, and it was a long time before they could bring themselves to move.

'Wait a minute,' shouted Pippi, and ran into the kitchen. She came out with two heart-shaped ginger-snaps. 'Would you like to try one?' she said. 'I don't s'pose it makes much difference if they're a *little* burnt.'

Then she went back to Tommy and Annika, who stood there staring and filled with wonder. And the policemen hurried back to the town and said to all the good mothers and fathers there that Pippi just wasn't quite suitable for a Children's Home. They didn't talk about having been up on the roof. 31

Everyone agreed that perhaps it was best to let Pippi stay in Villekulla Cottage. And if it should happen that she wanted to go to school, then she should arrange that herself.

But Pippi and Tommy and Annika had a really pleasant afternoon. They continued the interrupted tea-party. Pippi gobbled down fourteen ginger-snaps, and then she said, 'Those weren't what I'd call the *best* kind of policemen. No! Altogether too much silly talk about Children's Homes and pluttification and Lisbon.'

Later she lifted out the horse, and then all three of them rode on him. At first Annika was afraid and didn't want to, but when she saw what fun Tommy and Pippi were having she let Pippi lift her up on the horse's back too. And the horse trotted round and round the orchard, and Tommy sang, 'Here come the Swedes with a hullabaloo!'

When Tommy and Annika had crept into their beds that night, Tommy said, 'Annika, don't you think it's jolly that Pippi has moved here?'

'Of course I do,' said Annika.

'I don't even remember what we used to play before she came, do you?'

'Well, we played croquet and *that* sort of thing,' said Annika. 'But somehow it's lots more fun with Pippi, I think. And with horses and all that!'

Pippi Starts School

QUITE naturally, Tommy and Annika went to school. Each morning at eight o'clock they trudged away hand in hand with their school-books under their arms.

At that hour Pippi was usually to be found riding her horse or dressing Mr Nelson in his little costume. Or she would be doing her morning exercises, which consisted of standing bolt upright on the floor and then turning forty-three somersaults in the air, one right after the other. After this she would sit on the kitchen table and enjoy a big cup of coffee and a cheese sandwich in peace and quiet.

Tommy and Annika always looked wistfully towards Villekulla Cottage when they toiled away to school. They would much, much rather have gone to play with Pippi. If only Pippi had had to go to school too, it wouldn't have been quite so bad.

'Just think what fun we could have together on our way home from school,' said Tommy.

'Yes, and on the way there too,' Annika agreed.

The more they thought about it, the more it

seemed a pity that Pippi didn't go to school. Finally they decided to try and persuade her to begin.

'You can't *imagine* what a nice teacher we have,' said Tommy artfully to Pippi one afternoon when he and Annika were visiting Villekulla Cottage after having first done all their homework.

'Oh, if you *knew* what fun it is at school,' said Annika innocently. 'I should go out of my mind if I couldn't go!'

Pippi sat on a stool washing her feet in a tub. She didn't say anything, but just wiggled her toes a little so the water splashed around.

'One doesn't have to be there so *terribly* long,' continued Tommy. 'Just till two o'clock.'

'Yes, and we get Christmas holidays and Easter holidays and summer holidays,' said Annika.

Pippi bit her big toe thoughtfully, but didn't say anything. Suddenly, without hesitation, she tossed all the water out on the kitchen floor, so that Mr Nelson, who was sitting near by playing with a mirror, got his trousers absolutely soaked.

'Its unjust!' said Pippi sternly, without taking any notice of Mr Nelson's distress over the wet trousers. 'It's absolutely unjust. I'm not going to stand for it!' 35

'Not stand for what?' asked Tommy.

'In four months it's Christmas, and you'll be getting Christmas holidays. But me, what do I get?' Pippi's voice sounded gloomy. 'No Christmas holidays; not even the very teeniest Christmas holiday,' she complained. 'There's got to be a change here. Tomorrow I'm beginning school!'

Tommy and Annika clapped their hands with joy.

'Hurrah! Then we'll wait for you outside our gate at eight o'clock.'

'No, no,' said Pippi. 'I can't begin *that* early. And for that matter, I think I'll be riding to school.'

And she did. At exactly ten o'clock the next morning she lifted her horse down from the front porch, and a moment later all the people of the little town rushed to their windows to see what horse had run away. That is to say, they *thought* it had run away. But it hadn't. It was simply that Pippi was in a bit of a hurry to get to school. In a wild gallop she burst into the school-yard, hopped off the horse at full speed, tied him with a string, and flung open the door of the school-room with a terrific crash that made Tommy and Annika and their classmates jump in their seats.

'Hey, hurrah!' shouted Pippi and waved her big hat. 'Am I in time for pluttification?'

Tommy and Annika had explained to their teacher that a new girl called Pippi Longstocking would be coming. The teacher had also heard about Pippi from people in the town. As she was a very kind and pleasant teacher, she had decided to do everything she could to make Pippi feel at home in school.

Pippi flung herself down into an empty seat without anyone having asked her to do so. But the teacher took no notice of her careless manner. She just said in a friendly way, 'Welcome to school, little Pippi. I hope you will be happy here and that you will learn a great deal.'

'To be sure! And *I* hope I'll get Christmas holidays,' said Pippi. ' 'Cause that's the reason I've come. Justice above all things!'

'If you'll first tell me your full name,' said the teacher, 'I shall enrol you in the school.'

'My name is Pippilotta Provisionia Gaberdina Dandeliona Ephraimsdaughter Longstocking, daughter of Captain Ephraim Longstocking, formerly the terror of the seas, now Cannibal King. 37

Pippi is really just my nickname, 'cause my father thought Pippilotta was too long to say.'

'I see,' said the teacher. 'Well then, we shall call you Pippi too. But now perhaps we should test your knowledge a bit,' she continued. 'You're quite a big girl, so you probably know a great deal already. Let us begin with arithmetic. Now Pippi, can you tell me how much seven and five make?'

Pippi looked rather surprised and cross. Then she said, 'Well, if *you* don't know, don't think I'm going to work it out for you!'

All the children stared in horror at Pippi. The teacher explained to her that she wasn't to answer in that way at school. She wasn't to call the teacher just 'you' either; she was to call the teacher 'ma'am'.

'I'm awful sorry,' said Pippi apologetically. 'I didn't know that. I won't do it again.'

'No, I should hope not,' said the teacher. 'And now I'll tell you that seven and five make twelve.'

'You see!' said Pippi. 'You knew it all the time, so why did you ask, then? Oh, what a blockhead I am! Now I called you just "you" again. 'Scuse me,' she
38 said, giving her ear a powerful pinch.

The teacher decided to pretend that nothing was the matter.

'Now, Pippi, how much do you think eight and four make?'

'I s'pose round about sixty-seven?' said Pippi.

'Not at all,' said the teacher. 'Eight and four make twelve.'

'Now, now, my good woman, that's going too far,' said Pippi. 'You said yourself just now that it was seven and five that made twelve. There oughter be *some* order, even in a school. If you're so keen on this silly stuff, why don't you sit by yourself in a corner and count, and let us be in peace so we can play tag? Oh, dear! Now I said just "you" again,' she said with horror. 'Can you forgive me this last time too? I'll try to remember better from now on.'

The teacher said she would do so. But she thought that trying to teach Pippi any more arithmetic wasn't a good idea. She began to ask the other children instead.

'Can Tommy answer this question, please,' she said. 'If Lisa has seven apples and Axel has nine apples, how many apples have they together?'

'Yes, answer that one, Tommy,' Pippi chimed in. 39

'And at the same time answer me this one: If Lisa has a tummy ache and Axel has even *more* of a tummy ache, whose fault is it, and where had they pinched the apples?'

The teacher tried to look as if she hadn't heard, and turned to Annika.

'Now, Annika, this problem is for you: Gustav went with his friends on a school outing. He had elevenpence when he went and sevenpence when he came home. How much had he spent?'

'All right,' said Pippi, 'then *I'd* like to know why he was so extravagant, and if it was ginger beer he bought, and if he'd washed well behind his ears before he left home.'

The teacher decided to give up arithmetic completely. She thought that perhaps Pippi would be more interested in learning to read. She therefore brought out a picture of a pretty little green island surrounded by blue water. Just over the island stood the letter 'i'.

'Now, Pippi, I'm going to show you something very interesting,' she said quickly. 'This is a picture of an iiiiiiisland. And this letter above the iiiiiiisland is called "i".'

'Ow, I can hardly believe that,' said Pippi. 'It looks to me like a short line with a fly-speck over it. I'd like to know what islands and fly-specks have to do with each other.'

The teacher brought out the next picture, which was of a snake. She explained to Pippi that the letter over it was called 's'.

'Speaking of snakes,' said Pippi, 'I don't s'pose I'll ever forget the time I fought with a giant snake in India. It was such a horrid snake, you can't *imagine*; he was fourteen yards long and as angry as a bee, and every day he ate up five Indians and two little children for dessert. One day he came and wanted *me* for dessert, and he wound himself round me – krratch – but "I've learned a thing or two at sea," I said and hit him on the head – boom – and then he *hissed* – uiuiuiuiuiuitch – and then I hit him again – boom and – ow –, well – then he died. So *that's* the letter "s"? Very interesting!'

Pippi had to catch her breath for a moment. The teacher, who was beginning to think Pippi a noisy and troublesome child, decided to let the class draw for a while. Surely Pippi would sit quietly and draw, thought the teacher. So she brought out paper and pencils and handed them out to the children.

'You may draw whatever you like,' she said, and she sat down at her desk and began correcting copy-books. After a while she looked up to see how the children were getting on. They all sat looking at Pippi, who lay on the floor drawing to her heart's content.

'But, Pippi,' said the teacher impatiently, 'why don't you draw on the paper?'

'I used that up long ago. There isn't room enough for my whole horse on that silly little scrap of paper,' said Pippi. 'Just now I'm working on the front legs, but when I get to the tail I'll most likely be out in the corridor.'

The teacher thought hard for a moment. 'Per-haps we should sing a little song instead?' she suggested.

All the children stood up beside their seats; all but Pippi, who lay still on the floor.

'Go ahead and sing,' she said. 'I'm going to rest a bit. Too much study can break the healthiest.'

But now the teacher's patience had come to an 42 end. She told all the children to go out into the school-yard, because she wanted especially to talk to Pippi.

When the teacher and Pippi were alone, Pippi got up and came forward to the desk.

'Do you know,' she said, 'I mean, do you know, *ma'am*, it was really lots of fun to come here and see what it's like. But I don't think I want to go to school any more, Christmas holidays or no Christmas holidays. There's just too many apples and islands and snakes and all that. I just get flustered in the head. I hope you're not disappointed, ma'am.'

But the teacher said she *was* disappointed, most of all because Pippi wouldn't try to behave properly, and that no girl who behaved as badly as Pippi would be allowed to come to school even if she wanted to very much.

'Have I behaved badly?' asked Pippi, very surprised. 'But I didn't know that myself,' she said, looking sad. No one could look as tragic as Pippi when she was unhappy. She stood silently a minute, and then she said in a shaking voice, 'You understand, ma'am, that when your mother is an angel and your father a Cannibal King, and you've travelled all your life on the seas, you don't really know *how* you 43 oughter behave in a school with all the apples and the snakes.'

Then the teacher said that she quite understood, and that she wasn't disappointed in Pippi any longer, and that perhaps Pippi could come back to school when she was a bit older. And Pippi said, beaming with pleasure, 'I think you're awful nice, ma'am. And look what I've got for you, ma am!'

Out of her pocket Pippi brought a fine little gold chain, which she laid on the desk. The teacher said she couldn't accept such a valuable gift from Pippi, but then Pippi said, 'You have to! Else I'll come back again tomorrow, and *that* would be a pretty spectacle!'

Then Pippi rushed out into the school-yard and leaped upon the horse. All the children crowded around to pat the horse and to watch her leave.

'I'm glad I know about Argentine schools,' Pippi said in a superior manner looking down at the children. 'You ought to go *there*! They begin Easter holidays three days after Christmas holidays, and when the Easter holidays are over, it's just three days till summer holidays. Summer holidays are over on the
first of November. 'Course, then there's a bit of a

grind until Christmas holidays begin on the eleventh of November. But it's not too bad, 'cause at least there aren't any lessons. It's strictly forbidden to have lessons in Argentina. It does happen once in a while that some Argentine child or other hides himself in a cupboard and sits there in secret and reads, but woe betide him if his mother finds him out! They don't have arithmetic in the schools there at all, and if there's a child who knows how much seven and five is, he has to stand in the corner all day if he's so stupid that he tells it to the teacher. They have reading on Fridays only, and then only in case they happen to have some books there. But they never do.'

'Yes, but what do they do in school then?' asked a little boy.

'Eat sweets,' said Pippi without hesitation. 'A long pipe goes direct from a sweets factory in the neighbourhood to the school-room. Sweets shoot out of it all day, so the children are kept busy just eating.'

'But what does the teacher do?' asked a little girl.

'Picks the papers off the sweets, dunce,' said Pippi. 'Did you think they did it themselves? Hardly! They don't even as much as go to school themselves. They send their brothers.'

Pippi waved her big hat.

'Yoicks, tally ho!' she cried. 'You won't see me in a minute. But always remember how many apples Axel had, else you'll come to a bad end, hahaha!'

With ringing laughter Pippi rode out through the gate, so fast the gravel whirred around the horse's hooves and the school windows rattled.

Pippi Sits on the Gate and Climbs a Tree

OUTSIDE Villekulla Cottage sat Pippi, Tommy, and Annika. Pippi sat on one gatepost, Annika sat on the other gatepost, and Tommy sat on the gate. It was a warm and beautiful day towards the end of August. A pear tree, which grew by the gate, stretched its branches so far down that the children could sit and pick the ripest little yellow-red August pears with no trouble at all. They nibbled and munched, and spat the pear pips out on to the road.

Villekulla Cottage lay just where the little town ended and the countryside began, and where the street turned into a country road. The townspeople liked to go for walks out Villekulla way, for it was there the most beautiful surroundings lay.

While the children sat there eating pears, a girl came by on the road from the town. When she saw the children she stopped and asked, 'Have you seen my father pass by?'

'I don't know,' said Pippi. 'What did he look like? Did he have blue eyes?'

'Yes,' said the girl.

'Black hat and black shoes?'

'Yes, exactly,' said the girl eagerly.

'No, we haven't seen anyone like that,' said Pippi definitely.

The girl looked disappointed and went on without a word.

'Ahoy there!' Pippi shouted after her. 'Was he bald?'

'No, not in the least,' said the girl angrily.

'*That's* a bit of good luck for him!' said Pippi, and spat out a pear pip.

The girl hurried on, but then Pippi yelled, 'Did he have uncommon big ears that reached all the way down to his shoulders?'

'No,' said the girl, and then turned about, astonished. 'You don't mean to say you've seen a man walk by with ears as big as that?'

'I've never seen anyone walk with his ears,' said Pippi. 'Everybody *I* know walks with his feet.'

'Oof, but you're silly! I mean, have you really seen a man with ears that big?'

'No,' said Pippi. 'There *isn't* anybody with ears that big. Why, that would be absurd. How would it look? One simply can't have such big ears.

'At least, not in *this* country,' she added after a moment's thought. 'In China it's a little different. Once I saw a Chinaman in Shanghai. His ears were *so* big he could use them for a raincoat. When it rained, he just crept in under his ears and was warm and snug as could be. Not that the ears had such a rattling good time of it, you understand. If it was *specially* bad weather, he'd invite friends and acquaintances to pitch camp under his ears too. There they sat, singing their sorrowful songs while it poured down outside. They thought a lot of him because of his ears. Hai Shang was his name. You should have seen Hai Shang running to his work in the morning! He always came charging along at the last minute because he liked sleeping late so much, and you can't imagine how lovely it looked when he came running along with his ears like two big yellow sails behind him.'

The girl had stopped and now stood with open mouth listening to Pippi. And Tommy and Annika had quite forgotten about eating more pears. They were busy enough just listening.

'He had more children than he could count, and the smallest one was called Peter,' said Pippi.   49

'Yes, but a Chinese child *can't* be called Peter,' objected Tommy.

'That's just what his wife told him too. "A Chinese child *can't* be called Peter," she'd say. But Hai Shang was most *awf'ly* stubborn and he said that the baby would either be called Peter or else nothing at all. And then he sat down in a corner and pulled his ears over his head and just sulked. And so his wife had to give in, of course, and the child was called Peter.'

'Oh, indeed?' said Annika.

'It was the horridest child to be found in all Shanghai,' continued Pippi. 'So fussy with his food, that his mother was quite unhappy. You prob'ly know they eat birds' nests in China? Well, there sat the mother with a whole plateful of bird's nest to feed him. "So, little Peter," she'd say, "now we'll eat a great big bite of bird's nest just for Daddy." But Peter only just clamped his lips together and shook his head. In the end Hai Shang got so angry that he said no new food should be made for Peter before he'd eaten that bird's nest just for Daddy. And when Hai Shang said a thing, it was *so*. The same bird's nest was sent in and 50 out of the kitchen from May till October. On the fourteenth of July the mother asked couldn't she please give Peter a meat pie, but Hai Shang said no.'

'Nonsense,' said the girl on the road.

'Just what Hai Shang said,' continued Pippi. '"Nonsense!" he'd say. "There's no reason why a child can't eat bird's nest if he only stops being contrary." But Peter just clamped his lips together the whole time from May till October.'

'Yes, but how could he live, then?' said Tommy in amazement.

'He *couldn't* live,' said Pippi. 'He died. Of contrariness. The eighteenth of October. And buried the nineteenth. And on the twentieth a swallow flew in through the window and laid an egg in the bird's nest that stood on the table. So it didn't go to waste anyway. No harm done!' said Pippi gaily. Then she gazed thoughtfully at the girl who stood in the road looking simply bewildered.

'How odd you look,' said Pippi. 'Just why's that, now? You don't think, do you, that I'm sitting here telling untruths? What's that? Just say so in that case,' threatened Pippi, and rolled up her sleeves.

'No, no, not at all!' said the girl in alarm. 51

'I wouldn't say you're telling untruths, exactly, but . . .'

'No, no, not at all!' said Pippi. 'But that's just what I *am* doing. I'm telling fibs till my tongue's getting black, can't you see that? Do you really believe a child can live without food from May till October? 'Course, I know well enough they can manage nicely without food three, four months, but from May till October! Why, that's silly! You certainly ought to *know* that's not true. You shouldn't let people make you believe just anything they like.'

Then the girl went her way and didn't once turn around again.

'How simple people can be,' said Pippi to Tommy and Annika. 'From May till October! Why, that's just so *silly*!'

Then she yelled after the girl, 'No, we haven't seen any bald 'uns all day today. But yesterday seventeen of 'em went by. Arm in arm!'

Pippi's orchard was really delightful. It wasn't well looked after, to be sure, but there were lovely stretches of grass, which were never cut, and old rose-bushes full of white and yellow and pink roses. They

were not particularly fine roses, perhaps, but sweetly

scented. Quite a number of fruit-trees grew there too, and best of all, some old, old oaks and elms which were perfect for climbing.

Climbing-trees were sadly lacking in Tommy and Annika's orchard, and their mother was always rather afraid they would fall down and hurt themselves. For this reason, they hadn't done very much climbing in their day. But now Pippi said:

'What about climbing up in that oak over there?'

Tommy jumped down from the gate at once, delighted with the suggestion. Annika was a little more doubtful, but when she saw there were big bumps on the trunk that one could climb on, she too thought it would be fun to try.

A few yards from the ground the oak divided into two branches, and where it divided it was just like a little room. It wasn't long before all three children sat there. Over their heads the oak spread its crown of leaves like a big green ceiling.

'We could have tea here,' said Pippi. 'I'll pop in and make a drop.'

Tommy and Annika clapped their hands and shouted 'Hooray!'

It wasn't long before Pippi had tea ready. And she'd baked buns the day before. She stood under the oak and began tossing up teacups, and Tommy and Annika caught them. Now and then it was the *oak* that caught them, so that two teacups were broken. But Pippi ran in and fetched new ones. Then it was the buns' turn, and for a long while a cloud of buns whirled in the air. They, at least, didn't get broken. Finally Pippi climbed up with the teapot on her head. She had milk in a bottle in her pocket, and sugar in a little box.

Tommy and Annika thought that tea had never tasted as good before. They weren't allowed to drink tea every day, but only when they were invited out. And now, after all, they *were* invited out. Annika spilled a little tea in her lap; it was warm and wet at first, and then cold and wet, but it didn't matter at all, said Annika.

When they had finished, Pippi flung the cups down to the grass below.

'I want to see how well the china made nowadays wears,' she said. One cup and all three saucers held, strange as it seems. As for the teapot, only the spout
54 broke off.

All of a sudden, Pippi decided to climb a bit higher in the tree.

'Well, I never saw the likes of this before,' she shouted. 'The tree's hollow!'

Going right into the trunk there was a big hole, which the leaves had hidden from the children's eyes.

'Could I climb up and see too?' said Tommy. But there was no answer. 'Pippi, where are you?' he called uneasily.

Then they heard Pippi's voice, not above them, but far below. It sounded as if it were coming from under the ground.

'I'm inside the tree. It's hollow all the way to the ground. If I peep out through a little crack I can see the teapot on the grass outside.'

'But how are you going to get *up*?' shouted Annika.

'I never can,' said Pippi. 'I'll have to stand here till I get pensioned off. And you'll have to throw food to me through the hole up there. Five, six times a day.'

Annika began to cry.

'But why worry, why complain?' said Pippi. 'Come down here instead, you two. We can play that we're languishing in a dungeon.'

'Not on your life!' said Annika. And for safety's sake, she climbed down out of the tree altogether.

'Annika, I see you through the crack,' shouted Pippi. 'Don't step on the teapot! It's a good old *cosy* teapot that never did a body any harm. And it isn't *its* fault it hasn't a spout any more.'

Annika came up to the tree, and through a little crack she saw the very tip of Pippi's forefinger. This comforted her a great deal, but she was still anxious.

'Pippi, can't you really get up?' she asked.

Pippi's finger disappeared, and in the twinkling of an eye her face popped out through the hole up in the tree.

'Perhaps I can if I really try,' she said, holding the leaves out of the way with her hands.

'Is it that easy to come up?' said Tommy, who was still in the tree. 'Well, then I want to come down and languish a little.'

'Well, first,' said Pippi, 'I think we'll fetch a ladder.'

She crawled out of the hole and slid quickly to the ground. Then she ran to fetch a ladder, struggled with it up the tree, and stuck it down the hole.

Tommy was wildly excited and couldn't wait to go
down. It was quite a difficult climb up to the hole as

it was rather high, but Tommy was brave. He wasn't afraid to climb into that dark tree-trunk either. Annika saw him disappear, and she wondered if she would ever see him again. She tried to look in through the crack.

'Annika,' she heard Tommy's voice say, 'you can't imagine how wonderful it is here. You must come in too. It's not the least little bit dangerous when you have a ladder to climb on. If you do it just once, you'll never want to do anything else ever.'

'Are you *sure*?' said Annika.

'Absolutely sure,' said Tommy.

So Annika climbed up into the tree again with quaking legs, and Pippi helped her with the last difficult part. She shrank back a little when she saw how dark it was inside the trunk. But Pippi held her hand and encouraged her.

'Don't be afraid, Annika,' she heard Tommy say from inside. 'I can see your legs now, and I'll be sure to catch you if you should fall.'

Annika didn't fall, but came down safe and sound to Tommy. And in a minute, Pippi followed.

'Isn't this spiffing!' said Tommy.

And Annika had to admit that it was. It wasn't 57

nearly as dark as she had thought, because light came in through the crack. Annika went there to make sure that she too could see the teapot on the grass outside.

'We can have this for our hiding-place,' said Tommy. 'Nobody could possibly know we're in here. And if they come round here looking, we can see them through the crack. And *then* we'll laugh!'

'We can have a little stick to poke them with through the crack,' said Pippi. 'Then they'll think there are ghosts.'

With this thought the children became so happy they all three hugged one another. Then they heard the gong-gonging which rang before dinner at Tommy and Annika's home.

'How awful,' said Tommy. 'We have to go home now. But we'll come here tomorrow, as soon as we get home from school.'

'Do,' said Pippi.

So they climbed up the ladder, first Pippi, then Annika, and Tommy after. And then they climbed down the tree, first Pippi, then Annika, and Tommy after.

PENGUIN CHILDREN'S 60s